# Josette

By

Dr. Katherine E.A. Korkidis

StorytellerUK2021 Nominee

# Table of Contents

# Dedication of this Book

This book is dedicated to my sons Christopher Michael and Michael James and my husband Michael Gerard. It was with their support and patience that made writing of 'Josette' possible.

In addition to my father, Artemis John Korkidis, who taught me that it is never too late to pen a novel. To my mother, Sophie Korkidis, that left this world much too early. She would often tell us that life had many doors. When one would close many more doors would be there to open; doors we have not seen as yet. We just need to open ourselves up to the possibilities and when those doors do open for us to find the courage to walk through. Thank you, Mom, for opening up my eyes to those possibilities.

This book is also dedicated to all those that see their life as hopeless and dread the coming of tomorrow. Do not give up on tomorrow for its promise of true happiness is just beyond our view.

# Segment from the Book
# Chapter 2 - Edgecliff

It was here and now that I realized there was something different about me. A sense of not belonging seemed to follow me wherever I would go. I was truly different from everyone else at Edgecliff and this realization made me feel totally unsettled throughout my years there.

It became a habit of mine to go down to the sea that Edgecliff overlooked and gaze for hours at the turbulent waves as they beat wildly upon the shore. The icy frost of the foam and the warmth of the clear waters seemed to imply an almost natural contradiction; a harmonious interplay of two extremes. A persistent battle of two forces destined to exist in one body. Each fighting for its individual existence, yet each accepting and respecting the existence of the other. Truly we were one. The yoke of tradition rested upon my shoulders, as the spark of rebellion grew in my soul. Often the conflict would be overbearing, but their coexistence was inevitable.

# Prologue

The story begins with Josette at the age of 25 years old. She has just returned to her childhood home from a successful classical piano world tour. It is snowing outside. As she glances at the snow through the window of her childhood bedroom, she reflects upon her past. She begins with the events of her 8th and 9th birthday – a turning point in her life. During this time she loses the two most important people in her life, her mother and father. She is sent to live with an uncle, her father's brilliant yet reclusive brother. He is a classically trained pianist that has no interest in raising a young child. Josette lives a life of solitude and finds solace in music. The only gift he has given this child has been the gift of classical music. She accepts this gift and makes it her life's passion. Edgecliff is her home until she is accepted and enters the Academy of Music. There she meets a gifted, yet lonely man named Daniel that saved her as she does him. Although married, he is alone. Josette brings him back to life and in turn Daniel restores her faith in love. They fall deeply in love and care for each other. Daniel's wife, Priscilla, is a socialite whose life does not include

Daniel. Her father was well endowed financially and never would have chosen Daniel as his daughter's future groom. Daniel and Priscilla once were in love but their desires in life drew them apart. They never had children, although Daniel wished for it each and every day. Her life was filled with parties and other social obligations. The idea of a family, children, could never be imagined. If she did accept Daniel's desires, those children would have been devoid of a loving mother. These two separate lives continued for many years. Daniel built his prestigious Academy and focused on his music. She in turn built a strong foundation and presence in Society. They barely saw or spoke to each other. Josette and Daniel fell in love at first sight. Josette was a freshman at the Academy that barely spoke and was often alone. He took an interest in her and the rest developed. Priscilla knew of their love and was adamant about not allowing a divorce. It would disgrace her socially and would just not happen. Daniel, in turn, knew the price and was willing to pay it. Josette would not allow it. Upon graduation from the Academy, Josette left Daniel. She was accepted for a world tour for 5 years. Daniel's loss was so immense that he found solace at the bottom of a bottle. Eventually, Priscilla had no need for him and released him. But he has lost all, his position at the Academy, his career in music, his position in Society, his friends, and his home.

As Josette remembers all, she hears the voice again and now realizes it is Daniel calling her. The urgency in the voice compels her to find him. Homeless and living with no future, she takes him home. She helps him to become the man he once was. Their future together is now secure.

*Chapter 1*

# Remembrance

The snow fell silently upon the ground. The crystals seemed to dance upon the windowsill, each crystal displaying its uniqueness. Then as brilliantly as it dances for its ardent observers the snowflakes fell into oblivion in the mass of the snow below. The night was dark and gloomy. If it weren't for the streetlamp across the way, one would envision that bleak darkness only prevailed upon the earth. The streetlight reflected upon a small and slender shadow standing motionless in a window above the street. As the intensity of the light increased, aided by the slight brilliance of the moon peering through the storm, the shadow became a shape and form. She was a young girl, twenty-five years of age, petite, slender. Her long hair fell straight over her shoulders and its dark brilliance became more exuberant in the light cast upon it. Her checks were pale and drawn well into her face. Her features were ordinary except for her eyes. Big brown olives in the midst of soft white skin. Haunting with a mystery unique to themselves. Deep with the wisdom of the ages, yet sad for the miseries and sorrows of living. Those eyes told so much of life if only one took the time to read them. Her lips never told what her eyes revealed. She was quiet, never spoke. Often, she was called shy, a mouse, yet she could not speak to those who would not hear. Her existence was a secret to the world and would remain so for evermore.

The light shone upon her as she stood staring intensely into the night. Her eyes followed each snowflake sadly as it fell to the ground. As she looked intensely into the night her mind seems to drift deeper and deeper into thought, until all the sounds of the night blended into nothingness; and all that could be heard were her words to herself. "I find myself often gazing longingly out of a clear window. Staring down at the streets below, my eyes fixed upon strangers, people as they quickly pass my eye's view. I wonder about their lives, are they as dull and lifeless as is mine. And if they are, who is to blame. Is it life or is it the individual? Do we make our fate, or is it our fate that shapes us? A man hurries across the street barely missing an oncoming car. What stroke of luck compelled the man to suddenly notice the car in time to avoid collision? And what if he hadn't, what effect would his death have upon the world? Can one obscure little man change the course of history, the fate of mankind? And how much control do we have in the balance of things? Is every decision a crossroad with two paths, each lying on a fully predetermined road? Can we alter our fate or is it a path of no return? Then what lies out there for me. Is it possible that somewhere, someday I will find the happiness I have always longed for? And what will this source be and how long until I find it? So many unanswered questions that seem to lead to more and more questions. So many uncertainties but is not life itself a massive uncertainty. And if I fear uncertainty, then I fear life. Could I exist knowing what was to come, especially if it was bleak and dark. But the unknown to me has always been just as bleak, just as dark. If only there was something out there, even remotely optimistic, maybe I would not live in such fear. I would not dread awakening in the morning and happily welcoming the coming of night and sleep; sleep, a temporary rest from the misery of the day. Sometimes as I lay on my bed, my eyes fixed upon the ceiling, I pray that tomorrow would not come. That somehow by some miraculous process time would be dilated to the point of standing still for an eternity. Yet, time passes on into days and years, and every year blends into the next with no hope of a better tomorrow. My life has changed so drastically over the past few years, yet my spirit is as crushed today as it was then. My surroundings may change, but my feelings and this constant internal sorrow stay with me continuously. I cannot seem to arise above this depression. Every day of my life I feel the approach of disappointment and every day keeps its promise of such." These were the haunting thoughts that never seemed to depart, but lingered in Josette's mind always, and especially on this particular night. Her concentration was so intense, she barely heard "a voice calling" her – "Josette, Josette, come to me". She quickly gazed around the room almost to avoid what might be there. "Am I losing my mind", she thought out loud. Again, the voice called to her, this time louder than before, "Josette, Josette, come to me". She could not dismiss the urgency in the voice, yet her eyes could not find the source. As her eyes swept the room, her mind once again began to wander.

It was the eve of her 8th birthday when her father recreated her bedroom for his little angel. Being a carpenter by hobby, he carved each and every piece by hand adding exquisite detail. The dresser with it elegant handles, the backdrop to her bed, and her special multi-drawer secretariat desk with its Queen Anne legs. Every piece more beautiful than the next. Her pastime was her desk with the many hidden drawers where she would hide her treasurers from the world. She would sit for hours drawing on this very desk. Yet her favorite piece was an ornately carved wooden box now sitting dust fallen on this desk. All of Josette's pastimes seem to evolve around music. Her favorite toys were generally musical in their form. The child would sit silently for hours watching colorful clowns and dainty ballerinas dance to the lively waltzes by Strauss or to the minuet by Boccherini. Often her mother would surprise her with yet another unusual music box to add to her already rich collection; as she did on this particular day. As Josette playfully asked for her surprise, her mother gave her a fairly large box. She knew how Josette loved to open boxes, and she enjoyed watching the excitement and anticipation in her little darling's face. The box opened readily to expose an ordinary rectangular walnut form. It had ivory – like carvings on the top and sides that seem to add to the elegance of its rich brown tone. The front revealed two wood-laced doors and golden handles. The child reached and with both her hands, opened the doors to expose the interior. Her eyes filled with joy and surprise as she glanced into this box. The music seemed to surround her and its mellowness and serenity seemed to touch her soul. It was a beautiful ballerina dressed in ivory; her gown decorated pleasantly in gold. As Rachmaninoff's Rhapsody on Themes of Paganini (Variation 18) flowed from the box, one could see her pirouette gracefully around her escort in one swift motion. Josette was overcome by the beauty and tranquility of this box. No other toy had ever made her feel so secure, so relaxed, and so loved. She quickly ran to her mother, embraced her, kissed her; mother and daughter held each other tightly as they watched the couples in all its beauty bring the room to life.

This box with its haunting music was to bring comfort to Josette always, more so during her darkest moments. For it was within a year, on Josette's ninth birthday that her mother passed away. Everything she was suddenly gone and all that lingered on for both father and daughter were the memories of times past. A child somehow can never forget the closeness that she shared with her mother, and it seemed that this music box, her mother's last gift to her became the essence, the soul of the woman Josette loved so dearly.

Josette and her mother often would play a game together, she could see a little girl running to hide and her mother searching. A playful little laugh heard from behind the chair. As her mother found her she picked her up and embraced her lovingly in her bosom, as Mother and child gazed into each other's eyes. Their thoughts were communicated without words, their eyes revealed their deepest feelings. Truly this mother loved her only child, her daughter. The world was not hers to give, but what she did have she gladly gave to her darling Josette. No child was ever more loved. And no parent was ever more rewarded by such gratitude and sincere love.

She was a young mother yet an incredibly wise one, she knew the secrets of motherhood; love, compassion, and understanding, but more so she knew the meaning of the word devotion. But unkind as life can be it was so to her as well. On her daughter's 9th birthday, she passed away. Everything she was suddenly gone and all the lingered on for both father and daughter were the memories of time past. A child somehow can never forget the closeness that she shared with her mother. Now the abrupt loss of her mother while she embraced her was an unbearable shock for a little girl. Her mother died in the street returning from a local bakery. In her arms she embraced a large cake with writing – Happy Birthday to my Little Doll.

She heard the brakes of a car shrieking. She hurried to the window and as she gazed down at the street below, she saw her mother lying there – motionless. Quickly she ran outside through the curious crowd to her mother's side. Her mother still held the cake box lovingly to her chest.

Josette tore the box from her arms and flung it to the side. She placed her head upon her mother's bosom and could hear the last breaths her mother gave.

The blood from her head and body coated Josette's uniform so that the blue and white checks became a uniform red design. She clung to her mother although she knew that she was gone. Several people rushed to the child's aid and tried to separate her from her mother's body, yet in vain. She responded only to her father's voice and walked slowly to his side. She was not hysterical, nor troublesome. Just unusually quiet and succumb for a young child, especially one with the vitality of Josette. For the next few days Josette neither cried, laughed, nor spoke. She quietly sat by the window of her bedroom and stared down at the street below. In her mind she could still see her mother's blood staining the street. She could see her father with his swollen, tearful eyes and a few men in white carefully lifting her mother's body unto a stretcher and subsequently placing the stretcher into a standing ambulance. She could see the faces of the people busily talking and pointing to the blood stains. She saw their indifference although they all knew and respected her mother. Why do they not feel as I feel? Why are they not crying, she thought? She saw the man who killed her mother get into his car and drive away. Does he feel for what he has done? Why is he allowed to go free? Why I must truly suffer, she thought.

Gradually those happy, joyous eyes seemed to age and mature. Sadness and depression set in where laughter and joy once roamed.

As she sat there quietly thinking, she heard a weak tap upon her door. She turned to face her father, who had slowly made his way into the room. If a man ever appeared distort and totally broken, this man did. His eyes were red and swollen as if he had been crying for days. His appearance was that of a beggar who had managed to find a fine suit of clothes that somehow did not fit him properly. She always thought him to be a handsome man with a flair for color coordination in his attire. Yet somehow on this day his beauty seemed to have faded, and his neglect for his appearance was obvious.

"Please Josette speak to me. You are the only one that I have left in this world, I cannot lose you as well. Come back to me, smile for me just once more." He spoke yet in vain. She pitied him and tried so hard to say the words he wanted to hear. Yet she could not. She could only stare at him with those lifeless eyes. She tried to move her lips, to form a smile, still she could not. Somehow, she had lost control of her movements, and could not respond to his request, although she desperately wanted to. Slowly he turned around, walked out of the room, closing the door behind him, as he did for so many days. She wanted to run to him, scream and cry, tell him how much she loved and needed him, yet she could not. She was stiff and unable to move.

That afternoon, a man so full of life only just a few days past, put a gun to his head. Josette could not move as she heard the sound. A neighbor responded to the child's screams for she found her father lying on his desk. Within those few days this beautiful child, full of love, lost all that she loved. No one knew what to do for such a child and so she was moved to Edgecliff to live with an uncle, the brother to her father that she had never met, a musician that traveled the world. He had no time for a young child that needed to grieve. He had no time to hold and comfort her. And so Josette put all that pain away deep into her soul never to be released.

When she arrived at Edgecliff all seemed so large and dark.

# Chapter 2

# Edgecliff

An orphan's fate depends on those around them. At the age of 9, a guardian was still needed. Biology takes preference and so Josette was placed with her only living relative, her father's older brother Jonathan Harrington. He lived alone in a large stately mansion overlooking the sea on the edge of a cliff in coastal Maine. The estate was called "Edgecliff". It was a private estate with extensive grounds. Jonathan David Harrington, a bachelor, and a well-recognized concert pianist, was barely home. And when he was home, he kept to himself. His estate, his home, was maintained by many men and women that visited Edgecliff during the day but were never allowed to stay. Every evening as all left, he would retire to his room in the West wing, not to be seen again until morning. Josette would pretend he was a wicked being with no soul nor reflection. The child grew up with many strangers as companions, yet devoid of familial love. The East wing, Josette's home had a total of 22 rooms, most of which were locked except for one room, Josette's. She often wondered, as any young child, what lay behind those locked doors. The West wing possessed 30 more rooms that were occupied by her uncle. Guests rarely visited. Her uncle preferred the isolation. Edgecliff was his refuge and Josette's prison. She was allowed to walk the grounds and often did. The grounds were parklike and impeccably maintained. The parklike surroundings lead to a fountain immersed in the center of a green maze. To the left of the maze was an old English garden that seemed to go on forever. Flowers from remote places could be found there. Their fragrance seemed to sweep over the entire grounds. To the right of the maze was the Gazebo. Josette's favorite place to visit.

In the midst of this outside home was a large table with many chairs. Josette found her paradise. All that could be heard was the sweet sound of a lark and the crashing waves below. From the Gazebo on the edge of the grounds she could see down the cliff to the rocks below. She would often, as a young child, stand on the top of the table and pretend to jump off this cliff. She would wonder how it would feel to experience those few unique moments of falling and the sudden collision with the rocks below. Then she would come to her senses and descend the table. What would Mr. Harrington think, she would say out loud. Although her uncle she was still to always address him as Mr. Harrington. Once she forgot and spent three days locked in her room with no food nor drink. His hatred and cruelty toward his charge extended greatly and was seen on many occasions. Yet he gave her one gift – the gift of music. It was only when he played the grand piano in his music room that he was able to show her any kindness. It was almost as if the music would "soothe the savage beast", and he became human again. She learned with time not to anger the beast. If she dared to touch his possessions, her punishment would be worse than the one before. So, Josette kept to where and what she was allowed. Often, he would leave for his concert tours and Josette would be left alone for months at a time. Although she dreaded the isolation and loneliness that followed and feared when the dark set upon the mansion – she preferred his absence. It was on one such trip at the age of 12, that Josette found the courage to explore the West wing. At first her find was minimum, room upon room, all locked; even the room that belonged to her uncle. Eventually she came upon a room whose lock was old and needed repair. The room seemed well decorated and had a strong smell of jasmine and roses. Fresh yellow roses sat on a small drawing table in the center of the room. This room was so different from hers. It was bright and full of life. As she entered the bedroom past the sitting room, she saw a portrait on the wall. It was that of a young woman with delicate features, a beautiful face with eyes not unlike her own, and flowing auburn hair. On the young woman's finger was a stunning diamond ring. She stared at the portrait for a while wondering who this might be. There was a familiarity about this woman as if Josette once met her. Why was this portrait here, in this room where time stood still? Josette followed the beauty in those smiling eyes. The kindness in those eyes reflected that of Josette's mother. Could this be? Could this be a portrait of her mother? She could barely remember her, but those eyes could never be forgotten. No, she was being unrealistically hopeful; she quickly left the room with no further thought of this.

The next morning, she revisited the room in the hope that she could see those eyes more clearly and remember. Indeed, her hope became her reality. The only picture she had of her dear mother was truly the portrait she was now staring at. As she viewed all in this room, she realized she had seen all before. On a small table sat a music box, not unlike those in her own room. This was certainly her mother's room, but when and how. Did her mother live at Edgecliff, but why? So many questions with so few answers. She began to open drawers and cabinets in the hope of finding those needed answers. She searched throughout the room. Clothes in the closet and drawers clearly belonged to her mother. All was preserved and maintained. It was as if time stood still in this room. She could feel her mother's presence in all around her. There was a warmth here that brought her peace. It offset the darkness present in the rest of the house. The wallpaper was bright white with small lavender and rose flowers. It was a gentle yet colorful display. The curtains continued the colors with subtlety and taste. The bedspread did the same. These must have been chosen by Josette's mother. She now felt that closeness she longed for so long. In the corner on an upper shelf in the closet, Josette found an old journal. On the inside cover she saw the dedication, 'This is the journal of Elizabeth Ann Pemberton', dated five years before Josette's birth. She could not believe this was written by her long-lost mother. These words written on these pages reflected her mother's thoughts, wishes, and desires. Could this be the key into a woman she could barely remember, now only in her dreams. It was the writings of a young woman, barely twenty, a musician not unlike her uncle. She was a well-recognized cellist that played the cello since she was six years old. Josette knew a little about the cello from her fellow musicians. She knew it is a bowed string instrument with four strings tuned in perfect fifths. It is a member of the violin family of musical instruments. Josette loved all string musical instruments, but her passions lied with the piano and the harp, both of which she learned to play with time to perfection.

In the journal this young woman wrote how she loved to perform the Prelude from Bach's "Cello Suite No.1 in G", Gabriel Faure's "Après un rêve" (After a dream), Franz Schubert's "Ave Maria", and Dvorak's "Cello Concerto in B minor". These were her favorites. Josette wished she could have heard her play. Maybe she did play for her young daughter and Josette just could not remember.

This young cellist was set to marry her uncle, they were engaged. How could that be, a man Josette had learned to dislike. A man without a soul, yet he was described in these writings as one with much heart and kindness. What made this man change, Josette wondered? Josette continued to read as the hours passed. Night began to fall, and she was alone again, as each and every night. She quietly returned to her room leaving the journal in its resting place. Tomorrow her tutors would return, and she would have to wait until evening before she could visit the room again.

The hours seemed to linger forever for Josette. Of what use would science and math be when the window to her mother's life lay before her. Yet to her uncle studies were important and he followed Josette's performance over her many years at Edgecliff. Finally, the moment came and her tutors were gone. She rushed through dinner and ran to her mother's room. How wonderful it is to be in the midst of such serenity. She sat on her mother's desk chair and worked on her desk. She began to draw as she did when she was a child. She could feel her mother's love wrapped around her as she created a copy of the portrait on the wall. Time continued to flow until night came again. Josette fell asleep on her mother's desk. As the sun arose and a new day emerged, Josette quickly realized that this room was to be her refuge. She ran downstairs to meet her tutors once again. When her lessons were complete for the day, Josette raced to her new refuge. The thought of the journal further intrigued her. She began to read once again,

**<u>"Entry – June 29<sup>th</sup>"</u>** – Today Jonathan and I discussed our future together. He told me he cannot live without me. Somehow this thought does not comfort me, if anything it frightens me. I believe I care for Jonathan very deeply, but I do not believe I love him as deeply as he loves me. Yet he proposes to me every day. I continue to see Jonathan as a friend. He is such an intense young man; I am afraid I might hurt him deeply one day. I finally agreed to marry him and wear his ring. He was so excited that he invited his brother, his best friend, to Edgecliff to meet me. Tonight, his brother Michael arrives from London. Michael David Harrington was a well-respected international lawyer that had an excellent practice abroad. Jonathan so much wants us to meet. I hope he approves of me and allows me a continuance at Edgecliff for the summer and beyond, as originally planned by Jonathan.

**Goodnight, dear journal, until we meet again tomorrow.**

So this was the night my mother would meet my father for the first time, spoke Josette out loud. I must read on, she thought.

**<u>"Entry – June 30<sup>th</sup>"</u>** – I cannot believe what has happened to me, can it be love at first sight. I am always rational yet when Michael walked into the room, my eyes were fixed on him. A tall and thin young man with dashing dark brown hair and blue eyes that were fixed on me. He is indeed very handsome, and his smile gives such warmth. I knew he was the one, my future. I could see he felt the same way. But what of Jonathan? How can I tell him? What will he think of me? I am the woman he hopes to marry. Now I can become the woman who has betrayed him. I feel doomed to hurt someone as well as myself. Do I sacrifice my happiness, Michael's happiness, or that of my dearest friend? Do I have the right, the choice, to determine the fate, futures of all in this home? Can I betray and hurt my best friend? Yet

I know Michael is in my heart and somehow, I must make this happen without hurting Jonathan.

**Good night, dear journal, until we meet again tomorrow.**

<u>**"Entry – July 1ˢᵗ"**</u> – What a beautiful day, the sun is shining, and the sky is clear blue. Not a cloud to be seen. Jonathan surprised us both. Jonathan in his ultimate trust has made arrangements for Michael and me to spend the next few weeks together as he continues his world tour. "The pursuit of music waits for no one", he would often say as he left Edgecliff for yet another performance. He trusted Michael to keep me entertained. I pleaded with him to come along on this particular tour, yet he felt it was best if I stayed at Edgecliff. He did not wish to leave his brother alone without a companion. I felt as if he laid the foundation for what was to come. Jonathan left shortly after breakfast. I knew the next few weeks would be a true challenge and I must triumph. Jonathan must never know what is in my heart and my mind. Remember he is the man I am to marry.

**Good night, dear journal, until we meet again tomorrow.**

<u>**"Entry – July 2ⁿᵈ"**</u> – Today started beautifully and most promising. I could not imagine a better day. I asked to have my breakfast outside in the Gazebo, my favorite place on the grounds. As I arrived, I found Michael had asked to enjoy the morning in his favorite place. We talked about the coincidence and of our common interests. He was most interested in my music and requested that after dinner I

play my cello. We enjoyed the day together talking about our current lives and the future. The evening came and he requested his favorite piece - Franz Schubert's "Ave Maria".

He approached me as I finished and placed his hand gently on my shoulder. He kissed my check and said "the melody flowing from your cello seems to be coming from the heavens!!! The best I have ever heard so far!!! Bravissimo!!! As I stood up he hugged me with such warmth and gentleness I did not wish for him to ever let me go. As he closed in to kiss me, I pulled back. As much as I wanted this embrace and that kiss, I was just not ready. He quickly withdrew and apologized for his forwardness. I wanted to tell him it was fine with me, but I could not. I was engaged to Jonathan that is all that mattered.

**Good night, dear journal, until we meet again tomorrow.**

<u>"**Entry – July 3<sup>rd</sup> – July 6<sup>th</sup>**"</u> – For the next three days I saw very little if not at all of Michael. He was not at our favorite breakfast site and so I ate alone. He would leave early for the day and not return until late evening after I retired for the evening. I tried to adhere to his new arrangements but felt lonely and unloved. What if I reacted differently that first night would I now be happy? Yet the guilt lay raw. What must I do to make these weeks to become bearable? Finally, the evening of the 3<sup>rd</sup> day forced by hand. Michael came to me and asked me to play the cello for him one last time. He was to leave to return to London the very next morning. He was not to return to Edgecliff. I was devastated as if my heart was broken in two. How could I let this man, my

future, leave? At the end of my performance, he told me why he needed to leave sooner than planned. He told me how he fell in love with me the first moment we met. How my angelic music convinced him that he could not live without me. How he must leave to try to forget me. How he was embarrassed for making unreturned advances. I could no longer hold out. I explained to him why I moved away. I told him that I too was in love with him from that first moment we met. I too could not live without him and had every intention to tell Jonathan all when he returned.

This time Michael was taken by surprise. He approached me, put his arms gently around me and kissed me. This time I did not move away. I begged him to give me another chance and not leave. We held each other all night until the dawn.

**Good night, dear journal, until we meet again tomorrow.**

"<u>**Entry – July 7<sup>th</sup>**</u> – For the remaining weeks together we were constantly in each other's company. We spent every waking moment together learning more about each other. We spent every sleeping moment together in each other's' arms. I had removed the engagement ring given to me by Jonathan so I could feel secure in my choice. I knew Jonathan would return home soon and we must face him. But for now, all was well. The guilt slowly over time melted away. All that remained was the happiness I felt with Michael. I thought often maybe it would be best for the two of us to be gone when Jonathan returns. But how awful that would be. I owed Jonathan so much and I now owed him the truth about the both of us. We had not as yet completely crossed the line yet our deep feelings for each other could not be denied.

**Good night, dear journal, until we meet again tomorrow.**

Josette was so pleased to read about the romance between her Mom and Dad. She was grateful they found each other. Josette was born from a deep love between these two wonderful people. At the age of 12 she was still young but very mature at the same time. She realized the toll this love had on her parents and of course her uncle. She read all the entries but found herself fearful of ones to come.

"**Entry – August 1st** – Living the last month was like living a dream. If this is a dream, I wish to never wake up. If this is how romance with my one true love will be, then I yearn for each day to be the same as the last. I have never felt such happiness and such security. Yet it seems for us all happiness must come to an end for Jonathan returns today. I spoke with Michael this morning as to what would be best to do. I was willing to return to Jonathan if that would keep our family together. Michael felt he could not return to what we had before and if I examined my soul, I know it is true for me as well. So, we decided we must tell Jonathan together.

**Good night, dear journal, until we meet again tomorrow.**

"**Entry – August 1st (evening)/ August 2nd** – Last night was not a good night and today an even worse day.

Jonathan did not take it well, which I expected since he was betrayed by both of us, the two people he loved most in the world. The guilt, the pain, all returned for me. I never wanted to hurt my dearest friend and fiancé, Jonathan, not this way. He has done nothing but taken care of me, loved me, and given me everything I could possibly want. The pain in his eyes, his silence broke my heart. I started crying and could not stop. Michael was crying as well and begging for his forgiveness, but none was there to give. Jonathan slowly returned to his room without a word.

An hour went by and we began to worry. Jonathan always had such happiness in his eyes, now they were devoid of all feeling. Jonathan came home so excited to see us both and within hours we took that joy away to simply relieve our own guilt. I wanted to wait for a while before telling him, but Michael felt that was cruel and would prolong the inevitable. Michael was anxious and very uneasy. He has not seen Jonathan ever devoid of feeling. He was disturbingly concerned.

Over the next few minutes, he broke into Jonathan's room, not waiting for an invitation. Suicide by hanging is a common and terminal way for a man to die and the method chosen by Jonathan. As I screamed. Michael lowered Jonathan's body to the floor. He worked hard on reviving him and I called for emergency services. Jonathan was taken to the hospital within minutes. They were not sure if they could revive him, yet Michael's determination aided in keeping his brother alive. After what seemed like many hours, Jonathan, came to. We were allowed to see him, but he did not wish to see us. His last words to us both was "why did you let me live?" We never spoke again. As soon as Jonathan improved with the promise of not attempting suicide again, he was allowed to go home. He asked through his doctors that we are gone before he comes home. To give Jonathan the peace he needed we obeyed his wishes. Michael was concerned about another attempt, but a dear family friend promised to stay with him as long as he needed.

So, Michael and I left Edgecliff like two strangers in a dark stormy night. Not a word was said and we each went our separate ways. Michael back to London and I to New York for my next performance. We decided to give each other time and then revisit our future together.

**Good night, dear journal, until we meet again tomorrow.**

Josette was now drained by the intensity of her parents' relationship, but most of all, her uncle's experience. She decided to go to bed and fell quickly asleep. All her aspirations for her parents was now gone. Would they ever find their way back to each other? Although she knew the answer, the ending of that summer at Edgecliff seemed to suggest otherwise.

Six months went by and there was no further writings about Michael is her mother's journal. Josette began to feel somewhat delated. What has happened? How much time will it take?

**"Entry – February 1st** – I have been invited to teach the cello at the Royal Academy of Music, Britain's oldest music conservatoire, which is located in London, England. At first I was concerned about accepting. I did not wish to see Michael. Yet it is one of the finest places to teach music in England and such an honor to be invited as my first sabbatical. Founded in 1822 The Royal Academy of Music has provided training for both popular and classical musicians. Its former students include the conductor, Sir Simon Rattle as well as Sir Elton John and Annie Lennox. Sir Elton John calls the Academy "a place of sheer joy and exuberance, of meticulous artistry where talents are passed on from generation to generation." The Royal Academy of Music also serves as a link to music's tradition. Its museum collection includes instruments by Stradivari and the Amati family as well as manuscripts by Purcell, Handel and Vaughn Williams. And now it will include me. Michael and Jonathan always saw a natural talent in me that needed to be shared with young musicians. So, I answered yes. It would only be for a year and I would be exposed to the best musicians as colleagues in the world.

**Good night, dear journal, until we meet again tomorrow.**

**"Entry – February 6th** – I understand from mutual friends that Jonathan is doing well. Although he no longer smiles and I have been told that his temperament has changed for the worse, he has returned to the concert circuit. I was so glad to hear about the latter. I hope with time his temperament changes once again to that of my dearest friend. Well tomorrow I am off to London and the Royal Academy of Music. All my friends are excited for me and me for myself. Still no word from Michael but at this point I need to focus on my future.

**Good night, dear journal, until we meet again tomorrow.**

"**<u>Entry – February 7<sup>th</sup></u>** – The flight to London's Heathrow airport was not too long. I had so much paperwork to fill out for my first week of classes that I stayed awake and worked. It was all done by the time we landed. I will take a taxi straight to the Academy tomorrow morning to drop off all the paperwork I gave up sleep for. For now, I must stay awake for just a few more hours and check out my new flat.

I have flown abroad on several occasions and know to force myself to stay up the day I arrive, no short naps, sleep when night falls. The adjustment to time changes will be easier. My appointed 699 square feet 2-bedroom flat in Marylebone was within 0.15 miles walking distance of the Academy. Although I was close to the Academy, I still need to bring my cello which can get cumbersome so I will opt for a taxi the first day. Ultimately, I will take a chance and rent a car since my flat comes with a full garage. I love my flat. I have one full bedroom with a double bed and an additional bedroom one with a twin bed and a full well stocked kitchen. All including towels and daily maid service will be provided. I often thought of a perfect place as a blend of a hotel room and a flat. To make my life easier the Academy said they will provide a secure place in my classroom for my cello once classes begin. I was totally thrilled with all.

**Good night, dear journal, until we meet again tomorrow.**

"<u>**Entry – February 8th**</u> – I am so excited to be part of the faculty at the Academy I could not sleep last night. My brain was full of so many thoughts for now and the future. All my teaching strategies came to mind. Yet it would be best to meet the students first. I suspect they will be the best students I have every taught. They would not have been invited to the Academy if they were not serious musicians. The acceptance rate is 3% of all those who apply every year. As a teacher you never know what to accept from your student body, but an experienced teacher can create the perfect atmosphere for teaching/learning from the very first day. I enjoy inducing excitement on our first day together in my students of all the possibilities that are yet to be. I picked up my schedule today and I am teaching classes on the cello at various levels. I have an additional responsibility for chamber music and to perform at concerts, both internal and external. I spent the afternoon practicing to insure a wonderful 1st class for all my students.

I cannot wait to get started tomorrow morning.

**Good night, dear journal, until we meet again tomorrow.**

As Josette read the entries, she could not be prouder of her mother. A young woman, a Visiting Professor, invited to teach at the Royal Academy of Music in London. How awesome!! Yet her mother's career was not unlike the one she envisioned for her own. She too will be well recognized in her 20s in the world of music. Their instruments of choice will be different yet considered part of the string family, Josette's also had virtues of the percussion family, the piano. Yet for Josette at this young age, the separation of her parents was to be foremost on her mind. Her mother's focus was her career. She let six months simply vanish before she mentions Michael's name in her journal and almost one year after they met.

**"<u>Entry – July 8<sup>th</sup></u>** – I love each and every day I teach here. We are treated with such reverence and are so supported by students, parents, and most of all our administration. This evening I will be part of the strings section of a unique concert for me, more contemporary. I will be performing Titanic Life at the Royal Albert Hall as a part of a live orchestra for the 20th anniversary of the movie. The event will see the 1997 classic screened in high definition in the venue's iconic auditorium, as James Horner's timeless score is played live on stage by the Royal Philharmonic Concert Orchestra. A 95-piece orchestra and 40-strong choir will be filling the room with overwhelming intensity: cymbals crashing, strings swelling, horns attacking. Tonight, I will be one of the cellist of the Royal Philharmonic Orchestra. I am so proud to be part of this amazing Orchestra. The event went as planned. All the audience was in tears as was I and my fellow musicians. As I finished the performance and I was packing up my cello, a familiar voice asked if I needed help. A gentle hand was placed on my shoulder. As I turned our eyes met and it was Michael. I could not believe he was there. He asked if I had eaten and I said no. I never eat before a performance I said. And so, we went off together. Although I had classes the next day, we spent the night talking. It was as if time had never passed between us. His eyes looked as sad as mine when I first turned around. But now they were bright and sparkling as our days at Edgecliff. He had lost me, but now he found me once more. This time he was not to let go. As we parted the next morning, he said "Life is a gift and he has no intention of wasting it ever again". We will meet again tomorrow.

**Good night, dear journal, until we meet again tomorrow.**

<u>**"Entry – July 8<sup>th</sup>- December 8<sup>th</sup>**</u> –The next 5 months we were constantly together. Michael had met all my colleagues at the Academy, and they all loved him. I met all his friends at the firm and outside of the firm. We were inseparable. I have been the happiest I have ever been. On Christmas Eve after our seasonal concert Michael took me to an elegant restaurant, the Alain Ducasse at The Dorchester in London. The Dorchester is superbly located in the center of London, nestled between Royal Hyde Park and the historic streets of Mayfair. We were seated at the ***Table Lumière,*** located in the center of the restaurant, which is surrounded by 4,500 shimmering fiber optics, known as the Salon Prive, a 'cozy, private alcove'. He got down on one knee and asked me to marry him. Of course, I flew into his arms and said yes.

Josette closed the journal with a smile on her face. There were more entries but for Josette, the story of these two people was now secure. Her refuge remained but only for the weeks her uncle was gone. Over the next few months and years, she became more tolerant and understanding of this tormented man. With time they developed a strained friendship, but a friendship just the same. Jonathan never pursued the love of fatherhood for this young orphan, yet he would see to it that all that she needed was provided for. Her schooling, her lessons, her music were a part of her daily life. Josette put in all her effort to excel and excel she did. Social interactions were limited to the school halls. No friend was permitted to come to her uncle's home and in turn she was not permitted to spend time outside the home. Her interest in dating was nil yet a girl friend or two would have lightened her day. For Uncle Jonathan, human interactions were unimportant. Studies and music were sufficient to fulfill one's day, as he often told her.

And so, Josette continued to excel at both and by the age of seventeen she was admitted into the prestigious London Academy of Music to further her studies. Her uncle felt she was too young to study abroad alone. He insisted that she study her music locally and apply to the Academy upon graduation. Josette protested at first but realized that her benefactor could easily withhold her financial support, so she agreed.

# Chapter 3

# Passion for Music

The next four years encompassed heavy studies in music at the well-recognized distinguished school for the Arts, Juilliard, in the city of New York. Juilliard is a classical establishment in the center of the city at Lincoln Center. It was established in 1905 by Dr. Frank Damrosch. He established the Institute of Musical Art which later became Julliard. It is cited as the world leader in the areas of Music, Dance, and Drama. Over the years the music division became the largest program encompassing over 800 students enrolled. This program pulled students from over 44 states and over 42 countries. Areas of study available for Josette to choose from included historical performance, jazz, music performance, and opera studies. Several hundred part-time and full-time faculty members, Juilliard boasts of a three to one student-faculty ratio, allowing for a more intimate and personalized education. "The artists at Julliard appear in over 700 annual performances in the school's five theaters; at Lincoln Center's Alice Tully and David Geffen halls and at Carnegie Hall; as well as other venues around New York City, the country, and the world." Jonathan was proud of Josette's talents although he did not share his views with Josette. He would attend and record as any proud parent all her performances when he was not on tour. Yet he would be critical of every note that she would play. Never a proud word, only criticism and negativity. Josette worked even harder to prove him wrong. She was told she was gifted by so many, yet she yearned for his accolades, which never came. It is hard to live one's life waiting for that one moment of approval.

Josette spend her childhood and teen years in that state. Soon all of this yearning for acceptance would end as Josette was exposed to the world outside of Edgecliff.

To ensure Josette's focus and success she was not permitted to live on campus. Uncle Jonathan established a luxurious yet trendy urban residence at Lincoln Square within walking distance to Lincoln Center. Both Josette and her uncle shared this four-bedroom residence. On weekends Uncle Jonathan would return to Edgecliff by his private jet. Josette was left alone in the city to explore its offerings. During long weekends and breaks in semesters, Uncle Jonathan would insist that she accompany him to Edgecliff. Josette would schedule her performances during those breaks to insure she would remain in the city. She found comfort in those many lights as she gazed down on the city streets below. She would often walk around the outer terrace with its 360-degree view. On warm nights she would enjoy sitting and reading under the sky's extensive expanse.

# Chapter 4

# The Academy

Josette's first year at Julliard was indeed challenging. To complete her Music major in Piano Josette was required to complete 32 credits in classes such as Theory I: Diatonic Harmony, a course that provides an introduction to the theory and analysis of tonal music. In addition to her major requirements, Josette had to take two additional courses, namely, Juilliard Colloquium and Essentials of Entrepreneurship in the Arts. Each course was ½ of the semester and focused the students on the interrelationship of the artist and the community he/she serves. Each semester of her first year she had to take a Piano course, 15 hours of private instruction. A young professor was given the task to teach this particular course to Josette. He was a transfer for the Royal Academy of Music and was incredibly young for his education and experience. His name was Daniel John Ellington. He was tall, thin, with well received features. His flowing blonde hair was combed back and accented his handsome face. His mode of dress was that of a true professor. As Josette entered the room that first day, she noticed him, and he did the same with her. There was an immediate attraction yet neither understood nor pursued it. He was an excellent lecturer/pianist, and she enjoyed his class very much. His workload was fair and inviting in content. She could listen to his command of the piano for hours, well beyond the required 15 hours. He found her truly talented, and he knew very early on that with time Josette would far exceed the teacher. Over the next two years Josette and Daniel went beyond simply teacher and student, they were good friends. She worked hard on those 42 required credits and reached her senior year with beyond the 151 credits needed for graduation. She had amassed many hours of private instruction and had mastered the Piano far beyond her own expectations. Soon enough Josette became his only private student, and he became her mentor and career advisor. He became not unlike an agent and seeked out performances to advance her career. He helped her to create a Baroque/Classical style and to build her Classical repertoire. They were inseparable. They would often sit and talk well into the night. They shared all aspects of their lives and they had become one in their thoughts and desires. They realized with time that the feelings they shared were well beyond friendship, but they dared not proceed. Josette was his student; Daniel was her mentor. Josette was a student at Julliard and Daniel was married.

Josette had come to depend on Daniel for all aspects of her life. He was her mentor but more so her friend and protector. He was always there for her and her expectations were such.

It was her second performance at Carnegie Hall and the nerves had already began to take over her mind. As she began and stood on the stage she looked out onto the audience. There in the back of the room he stood quietly and unassuming. He simply smiled. As she smiled back, she knew it would be fine. Her performance continued flawlessly and with much merit. The smiles and applauds at the end, confirmed her success.

As the crowd began to move out of the room, she looked for him, yet he was gone. He was her strength, and he knew it; as did she. As they stared into each other's eyes for those few, but perfect moments, they were both renewed. It was as if for those moments the world around them had disappeared and their existence relied only on each other. This man, she barely knew, was her strength and her solace.

As the days progressed and she played at each concert hall her eyes would search for him, and he would appear. It was almost as a telepathic communique. He knew she needed him, and he was there. He would watch her intensely from a distance, and she would excel knowing he was there. A simple smile would connect them, and she would excel. Days became weeks, weeks became months, yet he was there. The audience between them would disappear, and they were alone staring into each other's eyes. Their connection was real, there was no doubt.

Yet one day all began to change. As he stood there staring at her, his gaze was not the same. He began to falter, to rest his eyes on another. Each concert, his eyes would move away. She knew all had changed, but she did not know why. Her strength began to dissipate, and she knew she would fail, if she did not focus on the task at hand. Time passed, and she had to rely on her own inner strength. He was there, but not in the same way. She did not know at the time that he was being watched and needed to protect her from the prying eyes and moving lips of others. For they did not speak to each other as yet; only gazed from a distance. They knew each other's desires and thoughts; at least that is what she believed. She felt a deep rejection, an uncertainty of what was to come. This unspoken bond was now changing. Did he no longer love her, want her? Did he begin to lose interest? Her heart was breaking more each and every day. How could he stare at others if he loved only her? She could not bear to look at him any longer. She would glance away, so as not to be hurt yet again. As she glanced away, his heart too began to break. Time passed and he just disappeared into the shadows. She would look up into the crowd and no longer see him there. There were days when her heart had become so heavy, she could barely breathe. She began to pour all her remaining strength and passion into her music. Each performance became better than the last. The applauds and accolades became greater. She was acclaimed throughout the musical world as a musical genius. Standing ovations after standing ovations became the norm; yet she felt empty, a sense of loss. When the music stopped, she felt her body fall into an abyss, only to emerge again the next day as a phoenix rising from the ashes. Her eyes would look for him every day, and each day be disappointed. They say that once in your lifetime you meet the one person you are destined to spend the rest of your life with. For that moment there is a connection, and the choice is ours to complete that connection or move on. But what if that person does not feel the same or at least does not see the potential. Then we move on alone wondering what might have been. Josette was convinced that this man was her destiny, her soulmate, yet he was so aloof, and often ignored her to speak with others after his performances. He adored the limelight and the accolades from so many. Josette was shy and could not go forcefully into the conversations around him. She stood off in the shadows and watched as others took first place. And so, after a few minutes she would walk away and be alone once again. Sometimes he would invite her into the conversation and sometimes he would ask her to leave. Both actions were equally capable of saddening Josette. He was her mentor and when they were alone, he was so different, relaxed, and more real. Around others he was a projection of what they expected him to be. Josette did not like this projection for it was not who he was. Over the last few months, they have been together as student and mentor and those months have been the best since her childhood days. She could not imagine a day without him. Her heart raced as he approached to meet her. She felt at ease yet very self- conscious. She wished to impress him and was devastated when she failed. He was not assigned to her at first, but they met at the library both reaching from the same book from either side of the bookshelf. Their hands touched and she knew. That afternoon he asked to be assigned as her mentor. They had met in a fortunate accident, or serendipity. It is one of Josette's favorite words. Now that magic was somehow gone except when they were alone. Yet once in your lifetime someone comes along that you are absolutely meant to be with. Every moment together feels perfect, the stars are aligned. The body and spirit are in balance. You are one. Those are the moments we hold on to and Josette was no different. She needed those fleeting moments to get through the next hour and the next day. Those moments were far in-between yet when they happened, they gave her life. What Josette did not realize at the time is that those moments gave him life as well. As much as he loved the accolades and the attention his fame brought him, he despised those times and searched for respite amongst the crowds. Josette was his hope for this much needed time. When he saw her face in the crowd his thoughts would drift to their times alone. Those moments when Josette saw him to be aloof were the moments, he relived with her. The sadness inside became greater and greater. One day upon that stage, she collapsed. The world rang with the news of her collapse. It was physical exhaustion, they would say, as she added more and more concerts to her time and rested less and less. Little did they know it was a broken heart. He ran to her bedside to simply hold her hand and gaze into her hazel eyes once more. He took the chance of exposing her to the gossip he had worked so hard to protect her from; but he could not stay away. She needed him now and he needed to be there.

For those few moments, she knew she was wrong about him. He still loved and cared for her. Yet neither dared to declare their love for the other. She so regretted with time that loss. Life is indeed unpredictable, yet wondrous; and to never take a risk, especially in the realm of human emotions, is such a loss. Yet we are all desperately afraid of uncertainty. It is the fear of exposing one's inner most thoughts that must be overcome, so as to allow one the courage to take the risk. Soon enough that moment would come, but not today. That brief visit renewed her strength once again. She returned to the stage with even more vigor that before; knowing in her mind and heart that he indeed still loved her.

# Chapter 5

# Daniel

Dr. Daniel John Ellington was born into wealth, position, and opportunity. His father, Jonathan Edward Ellington was a well-recognized and respected member of the upper class, a solicitor of good standing. His mother, Katherine Ann Elliott, an admired socialite, valued her family over societal standing. She married her husband as per the instructions of her father but with time and constant kindness she realized how much she loved this man. Their son became the center of her world and his. They showered their only child with much love and devotion. He had more than any child wanted or needed. From a young age Daniel showed much gratitude for this gift, his loving parents, He displayed many talents. In turn his parents offered him opportunities to showcase those talents and excel. He was a virtuoso at the tender age of seven years. Although his father hoped to one day pass on his practice to his son, Daniel's interests and talents led him to a different future. Daniel's mother saw his love for music to be not unlike her own, so she encouraged and nurtured it. Daniel was sent to the Academy of Music even though he was of a young age. He continued his musical studies into young adulthood. He traveled and performed often on the world stage. As a handsome and exceptionally talented young man he was often pursued by the fairer sex, but his focus was only his music. Members of his extended family saw his life as frivolous and without direction. Yet his parents were often in attendance at his performances to cheer him on and support him. Daniel was the perfect son, and they were the perfect parents. So, son and parents carried on together to create a future for their only child. Often time has a way to alter our course in life. It was shortly after his 18th birthday that Daniel lost his constant support, his mother. They say she died quietly in her sleep. This elegant, graceful, loving, "plein de vie" woman was now still forever. His father was devasted and said to never had been the same. The loss of his beloved wife was more than he could handle. He too passed two years later from a "broken heart". Daniel's world had fallen apart. His father saw to it that Daniel would be well taken care of and set as his only inheritor. Although family did intervene at first their contesting was irrelevant, the will was upheld. So, this young man at the age of 20 years being wealthy, handsome, and belonging to the "right" class became an attraction to all young debutants of the region. After the loss of his parents Daniel focused on continuing his education to acquire a doctorate in music and even more intensely on his career. He was determined to succeed yet his kindness opened him up to a potential loss.

A highly gifted young man, shy and soft spoken and often gullible, he allowed himself to be easily manipulated by his world. He did not choose to invest in financial endeavors but instead invested his time and finances to aid the poor and vulnerable. He chose to continue the works of his mother with his faith as his guide. One day at the age of 21 years he met a woman that shared his love for hard work and for the less fortunate. Her name was Elizabeth Grace Norrington. She was an older handsome woman in her mid-forties that often reminded Daniel of his mother. Elizabeth had two daughters, one of marriageable age. The youngest, Anna, a girl of 16 years, would often help her mother in service to others. She had a love for all around her and wish to make a difference. Elizabeth's eldest daughter, Priscilla chose other distractions at the age of 21. What Priscilla lacked in heart she made up in beauty and elegance. Daniel was instantly drawn to Priscilla, to her beauty and her "joie de vivre". He was captivated and could not resist. Elizabeth was pleased to have this particular young man interested in her frivolous daughter, so she agreed to the courtship. Their courtship was to last for one year, followed by an engagement and soon thereafter marriage. All was arranged. Although Daniel was not sure as to his own desires, without parents to support and guide him he trusted Elizabeth and Priscilla to decide his future. He wanted to further advance his career and having a wife of high social standing would not be a deterrent. If anything, it would open doors. Priscilla's father was active in the arts and on the Board of Directors of the Academy of Music. For Priscilla being linked to such a well to do and respected family would only serve to increase her current social standing. So, all was arranged. Was true love a factor in this arrangement early on, it was hard to tell. Daniel and Priscilla both had their reasons for the union, but mutual love did not seem to contribute. As time went on the choice to have a family was taken away from Daniel. Priscilla would not allow herself to be a mother. "Too boring" she would often say. So, Daniel accepted his wife's role in society and focused on his career. They barely saw each other and were married in name only. He was alone often but he preferred it for when they were together, the coldness between them was unbearable. He began to feel trapped in a web of his own creation with no way out. And so, Daniel continued his loveless life.

Although married for many years, Daniel was constantly alone. Josette brings him back to life and in turn Daniel restores her faith in love. They fall deeply in love and care for each other. With Josette in his life within one year's time Daniel excels and was promoted to Director of the Music Division as well as Deputy Dean of the college. By the time Josette graduates from Julliard Daniel had received many more promotions. His position on the day of her graduation was given as Provost and Dean of Julliard. His position at the college allowed him to play concerts together with Josette. During her junior year he organized her first musical tour. He accompanied her and they spent every moment together. If he was not playing, he would stand at the end of the hall in plain sight. She would look up and see him. Once their eyes met, she knew all would be well. She played every piece with passion and perfection. Daniel had decided that once Josette was ready to graduate, he would propose. He could not imagine a future without Josette. She was his muse and he hers. So Daniel decided the time was finally there and he made arrangement to visit his wife to ask for a divorce.

# Chapter 6

# Separate Lives

Sometimes you want so very much to believe that someone has changed, that you accept a temporary departure from their normal behavior as a major breakthrough. Yet sooner or later the day comes, and you know that the minor change was nothing more than a momentary displacement in time, which time has subsequently corrected. We can never delude ourselves with the thoughts that people will change, or more appropriately that someone will change because we wish her to do so. Change must come from within ourselves, and if she does not wish to do so she will always remain exactly the way she is much to our disappointment. Accepting this is accepting cold reality as it is. We all have images of what we would like to be or what we would like others to be. But rather than fabricating these images and trying to sustain them, maybe we should be tearing them down and closely observe the actual personality we are dealing with. If it is our own and we dislike it, then we have the right and opportunity to improve upon it or change it. But if it is another person we are observing, we must either accept her as she is or leave her. The cruelest thing we can do to ourselves as well as to her is to try to change her, for that is truly a hopeless battle that will successfully end in only crushing the spirits of both people involved. What is it about marriage that seems to bring out this need in so many of us? Daniel obviously married Priscilla for some reason that could have been love, yet he woke up one morning, looked into her face and was suddenly repulsed by what he saw. He felt she was no longer the woman he married, but some poor facsimile that he must immediately help to change back. But change back to what, back to some false image of the woman he believed he married. But she has always been the same from the very beginning and will always remain so. Yet day in and day out from this time forward he had placed total effort into this ludicrous endeavor. She had disappointed him by being herself and failing his pedestal image of her. Her revenge for his failure to see the truth, a life of never- ending misery. For Priscilla, his misery is of no consequence. He does not matter to her.

Daniel's wife, Priscilla, is a socialite whose life does not include Daniel. Her father was well endowed financially and never would have chosen Daniel as his daughter's future groom. Daniel and Priscilla once were in love but their desires in life drew them apart. They never had children, although Daniel wished for it each and every day. Her life was filled with parties and other social obligations. The idea of a family, children, could never be imagined. If she did accept Daniel's desires, those children would have been devoid of a loving mother. These two separate lives continued for many years. Daniel built his prestigious Academy and focused on his music. She in turn built a strong foundation and presence in Society. They barely saw or spoke to each other. Josette and Daniel fell in love at first sight. Josette was a freshman at the Academy that barely spoke and was often alone. He took an interest in her and the rest developed.

How is it that two people that are indeed soul mates can find a way to constantly miscommunicate? Such was the case with Daniel and Josette. Each time she would reach out to him, he would reject her. The pain would cause her to retreat in rejection. It took months, so much lost time, for the moment when they finally knew their future together was meant to be. You see Daniel was married and Josette respected him too much to interfere. In turn, Daniel knew that Josette was committed to her music and would not be the one to take her away from her passion. So, the moment finally came when the dam would no longer hold back their strong waves of emotion. They held each other and declared their deep love. They kissed for the first time and knew this must go forward at all cost. Josette's abundant love so well kept locked up for so long is now flowing continuously. But not like a gentle trickling brook, but like a massive river, robustly flowing downhill guided by only gravity into a tranquil valley. Daniel feeling the need for so much is wadding carelessly into this river and is unaware he cannot swim.

Priscilla knew of their love and was adamant about not allowing a divorce. It would disgrace her socially and would just not happen. Daniel, in turn, knew the price and was willing to pay it. Josette would not allow it. Upon graduation from the Academy, Josette left Daniel. She was accepted for a world tour for 5 years. Daniel's loss was so immense that he found solace at the bottom of a bottle. Eventually, Priscilla had no need for him and released him. But he has lost all, his position at the Academy, his career in music, his position in Society, his friends, and his home.

# Chapter 7

# The Beauty of Love

It is a funny emotion this feeling they call love. It is one of frustration, desperation, ultimate joy, ebullition, and completeness. At times one strays from the lower depths of depression to the soaring heights of happiness. Stability is dead. The emotions of the being are no longer controllable. One's sense of reason is gone. Events once understood, are now misconstrued. These events, normal to objective observers, become deeds of revenge, guilt, of rejection. The lover observes the world with one eye closed, carefully, yet with blinders on. He loves, yet he doubts. He judges, criticizes without cause nor reason. His loved one shifts from the element of his happiness to the element of his despair. He loves and hates simultaneously. He is the most confused being upon the face of the earth. How can one so confused ever be rationale? The emotions are equally unstable. To love and be loved in return is to be the rarest of all experiences. Yet with this experience comes the doubt of the unknown. Does your loved one feel truly as you do? Does he suffer greatly when you are apart? Can he obtain the state of restfulness when you are not with him? Can you feel like this for evermore? When can you relax? Is taking it one day at a time the only solution? Doubts, questions, encompass your life, yet no apparent comfort can be obtained through their answers. Your life is now one continuous stream of questions, an enormous question mark. No longer can tomorrow seem wanted, anticipated. For tomorrow brings a further element of the unknown. It only feeds the fear of the lover and becomes unbearable. Yet, with all of this there is no better experience than true love. The ecstasy of loving and being loved in return has no equal. The tender kiss that encompasses your body. The wonderous feeling you feel deep inside when you are held so close. The contentment, the warmth emanating from within when you lover holds your hand. It is a whole new world that one believed could truly never exist, yet it does for these unique beings – lovers.

To love is to sacrifice and Josette had sacrificed her soul for Daniel. For four years she loved only him, but he never truly knew. Although, at times he would approach her, speak to her, touch her, although she knew of his attraction towards her, she never returned any emotion. How could she, he was married. She loved him too much to put him through the scandal and misery of a divorce. She could never tell him of her feelings for she knew that he would run to her side. Their attraction was too strong, yet she must be strong for both of them. When they were alone, she could feel the intense emotion between them. Then he would reach out and touch her shoulder with his gentle fingers. Her soul, her very being would begin to tremble, but she would grasp hold of herself. She must not lose control. He must not see what she feels. How she longs to place her hand in his, to gently caress his hands with hers, yet she does not dare. Swiftly he removes his hands off her shoulder and his blue eyes fill to their depth with depression. If only she could comfort him. If only she could touch his face. How often she has done so in her dreams. Every night she dreams of confessing her secret love to him, of him gently embracing her and sweetly telling her of his love for her. Forget the world for we are lovers, and surely the world would disappear leaving them behind, together, forever. Yet, when she awakes, he is not by her side. He is lying with another woman and the darkness of her empty room confirms her realization that she is alone. With the coming of the dawn comes the hope that she will soon see him again. She hurries to the academy, and to the realization of her hopes. As she enters the main room, he is there waiting for her. During the course of the day, he is constantly asking to see her privately in his quarters. He notices everything she does or wears. He feels what she feels, he knows what she knows. Sometimes he looks into her eyes and she into his and they know what each other feels and thinks. When she is depressed, he is always there to comfort her. When she is alone, he is always there to protect her. She thinks of him and he appears. She does not understand it but she has never felt for anyone what she feels for him. She did not believe she could ever feel love again. She knew she loved him since the first day she walked into his music class four years ago. As he lectured that day, she could not help but stare at those wondrously blue eyes. She remembers as if it was yesterday, and she was eighteen years old once again. She remembers how he stared back and how his stare seemed to burn her soul. Soon they became friends, a friendship such as she has never known before. Before she knew it she was in love for the first time in her life. There were no bells ringing, as one customarily expects when one falls in love, no, just a quiet kind of happiness, contentment when they were together. Alas, she approached her final year at the music academy and the realization that she was to leave him, caused her to fall into a deep depression. For four years they were never lovers, except in her dreams, yet she knew when she awoke, she was to see him that day, so all was well. Now the fear that she could never see him again became overwhelming. Josette could not face a day without him. He was a handsome young man to many but to Josette he was a god. Deep blue eyes that told of the miseries of life, profound and mature eyes not unlike Josette's. His hair was golden as the sunrise over the meadow with ringlets intertwined one within the other. If Apollo were to view him surely, he would be envious of his beauty. His figure was sleek and well proportioned. He was tall and well built, yet when he placed her hand in his, his touch was gentle and compassionate. When he placed his fingers upon the keys of the piano, the magic of his music seemed to flow from the instrument in one steady motion and slowly touch her soul. His music spun a golden pathway upon which their souls would journey, meet, caress, and become one. The arpeggios began to run one into the other until their distinctiveness no longer existed. She was carried away upon the notes and brought to a state of tranquility, happiness, and inner peace. Then the music would stop, and she would return to her god, wholly renewed. And he would embrace her gently and together they would escape to a world of their own. She was petite and meek, yet she could never fear him. When he embraced her, all ugliness and pain seemed to melt as the newly fallen snow upon the ground.

*Chapter 8*

# A Woman without a Soul

Often when she thinks back upon the day she left the academy so many years ago, a tear begins to form in the corner of her eye. Immediately her intellect takes over and restrains her from proceeding down a futile road. How can one ever regain that which is lost forever? It gets a lot easier to restrain herself with the passing of time. You see she is immune to feeling now. She feels no compassion, no pity, no love for another, nothing at all for she is empty inside. Nothing touches her any longer and nothing will ever again. She will not allow herself to feel, it is not fair. Anyway, how can she feel when her soul died on the day she left him.

The last time she felt gaiety, laughter, and a love for life, she was too young to fully comprehend it. Even in her love for Daniel she suffered greatly. Now she smiles at everyone she meets, but the smile is far from sincere. It is a "mechanical smile", that she manufactured, so that she can turn it on or off at will. She walks and talks without feeling. An emotionless being living day in and day out amongst so call human beings. Truly a freak in other's eyes. People no longer interested her. Every day was like the next and the one before, every year was like the next. One continuous flow, days, years, are no longer distinct entities, just torturous continuities in time, that she adheres to. She works, but with a lack of enthusiasm. She works well at her music and for many hours at a time. They say work relieves the burdens of the mind, but what if those burdens once deeply implanted in one's brain have surfaced and interrupt your daily thoughts. Work then becomes a pastime in a futile existence. Futile existence is how Josette sees her life, and how it will always remain if she is to be without Daniel. The extent of her depression might be considered dangerous by those around her, almost suicidal. Yet she cannot put an end to her life, not now, not ever. Life is too precious and unpredictable. What might seem hopeless today can emerge as hopeful in the future. Getting through the sadness and despair is difficult but it will ultimately give you strength to endure. Josette cannot die and that is the plain truth of it. It is not the losing of life that she fears, no, Josette is never inhibited by that fear. She has seen too much of death to fear it. She must live to fulfill their dreams for her music. She owes that much to her parents. Their dream became her dream, and it must come true. This is the emotional truth that guides Josette and shall ever do so. She has her emotions well under lock and key, she will not feel ever again. No one shall unlock her heart least of all herself, she does not deserve the right. Her morals kept her and Daniel from happiness and she is to blame for her misery. Destiny by her rationale and intellect is the only right she grants herself, nothing more, nothing less. Indifference is the only game worth playing, she was taught well by people. One always draws the ace, and no one ever gets hurt. Unfeeling, unloved, and unknown. How sweet and funny it all appears. If Josette could laugh at her predicament, she would. But she cannot. All she can do is smile until there no longer is anyone there.

She does not pretend with herself, instead she is always honest with herself. She needs to play a role, a game with society. She must fulfill her purpose, but without Daniel to reinforce her dream, it is only partially there. Sometimes she looks ahead and sees cold, dark, gray dust, and then the cold dampness disappears, light shimmers through a niche in the darkness, and her dream begins to bloom. But soon enough the spring is gone, as suddenly as it came, and only the gloom of the winter remains to be her companion. Josette returned to writing in her journal as a way to control this loneliness and darkness that seemed to be her constant companion.

Josette's Journal Entry:

The events of the past few years have taught me much. The events of the past few days even more. When we are young, most of us believe we can map out the course of our future and achieve our goals with determination and hard work. I was indeed a strong believer and for many years my life followed suit. As we grow older, we understand that life is full of the unexpected and often life changing twists and turns. My father use to say to me when I was a child that "the one thing we can expect of life is the unexpected". But if we cannot control events, we can at least control ourselves, our reaction to those events, and meet the change with resilience and integrity. I have spent the months of this summer, I am ashamed to say, as a victim of my circumstances. I have now chosen not to adhere to this role any longer. Adversity can bring strength to accomplish much more than just survive. That "that does not kill us makes us stronger", a well-recognized phrase. My rationale dictates that these events of the past few days cannot be, yet my heart tells me otherwise. There is so much as mortals that we do not understand. "There are more things in heaven and earth, Horatio, than are dreamt of in your philosophy". A phrase from Hamlet that is always present in my mind. I must accept it for what it is, put my rationale aside, and follow its purpose. I now choose to pursue my music with more resilience and purpose than ever before, where this will take me, I do not know. My father would sit for hours at his secretariat desk writing often into the night. I have brought this desk back with me and will use it as transition into his world, now my world. I have placed the desk in my bedroom sitting room by the window. Although I do not face my father's view, I face the beauty of the woods surrounding my home. My muse has changed, yet still as strong.

---

Josette had a natural talent for the piano. After attending a concert with Vladimir Horowitz, a Russian-born, American classical pianist and composer, her interest in the piano emerged. She informed her parents that she wanted to be a pianist. At the age of 5 years old she began studying the piano with the encouragement of her mother, herself an accomplished musician on the cello. At the age of 10, she was thrilled to study under Mr. Horowitz, who lived most of his life in the United States and was widely regarded as one of the greatest pianists of all time. By the age of 16 with the insistence and support of her uncle Jonathan, she did her first performance at Carnegie Hall. She entered the Julliard School in New York City two years later. Josette was known by her fellow musicians as an intense young performer that would often practice for hours into the early morning. Her dedication to her art allowed her to be the only pianist at Julliard to be given 1st selection to study further under the famed pianist Rosina Lhevinne, a teacher at Julliard. Rosina gave up her ambitions to be a solo performer to avoid clashing with her husband Josef's career as a concert pianist. She was a brilliant teacher and spent much time bringing her gifted students to life. As

Josette won competition after competition including the famous Leventritt her fame extended throughout the US. The Leventritt Competition was a highly prestigious international competition for classical pianists and violinists. It was founded in 1939 by the Edgar M. Leventritt Foundation Inc. of Cold Spring, New York, in memory of jurist Edgar M. Leventritt. It was held in New York City, but this competition was not well known for it did not look for publicly but rather would set higher standards for its award recipients over all other competitions. The Leventritt award was sparingly given, and there was no award presented if the judges felt the required standard was not achieved. By the time Josette graduated from Julliard she had played with symphonies throughout most of the major US cities and Canada. After her graduation from Juilliard's Academy of Music, her international popularity led to a world tour beginning in Europe and continuing into the Far East. It was often written of Josette, "her command of the piano has an energy, scale, and sweep that a listener, once he had experienced it could never forget its beauty". Josette returned to Vladimir Horowitz as her mentor and guide of her career during her Academy years and beyond until his death. He accompanied her throughout Europe beginning with Holland and ending with Vienna. It was his support and friendship that kept her going with each performance being better than the last. The most successful international tour for Josette kicked off that summer with 21 concerts in 35 nights slotted for venues in Norway, Denmark, Sweden, Finland, and Russia. As it was her custom, Josette would tailor her program to the countries she visited. Because she was playing half the concerts in Russia, the program feature Rachmaninoff as well as Edvard Grieg, the national composer of Norway. Josette was invited to perform at the major concert halls throughout Europe. Such as the Wiener Musikverein, the concert hall in the Innere Stadt borough of Vienna, Austria, known as the home of the Vienna Philharmonic. The acoustics of the "Great Hall" had earned its recognition alongside concert halls including Berlin's Konzerthaus, and the Concertgebouw in Amsterdam. Josette had performed at all of them. She was often invited to perform at both national and personal events by royalty and dignitaries. Her most recent and unusual event was to perform Johannes Brahms "Piano Concerto No. 2 in B-flat Major" for the 40th anniversary of the Prime Minister of Belgium at the Sint-Baafs Cathedral in Ghent, the fourth largest and most beautiful city in the Flemish Providence. A special piano was brought into the cathedral for her performance with a full orchestra. Her reputation in Europe proceeded her and the expectations were often surpassed. Throughout her years abroad she was honored with many awards for her performances.

She would return from one tour, rest for a week or two, only to return to touring again. She was relentless and with each tour her fame spread. She was barely out of Julliard and had already toured the world several times over. She would spend much of the year on tour, though some extended engagements in major cities may allow for a certain degree of stability. Her life was practicing and performing for many years. On occasion she would return to the home of her early years, which she now owned, during her week in between tours. This was one such week. She would often sit in the darkness.

The silence of her empty room seemed to encompass her completely and rigidly. She extended her hand to a small box on her dresser. As she gently opened it, sweet melodious music began to pour into the room. Quietly it filled her being with a sad, yet passive sense of contentment. But somehow the music changed. It was no longer quiet and gentile, Chopin's Etude transformed mysteriously into Tchaikovsky's "Serenade is C Major", Opus 48, 63$^{rd}$ movement, the "Elegy". The Elegy's softly dissonant beginning was incredibly beautiful. The music played continuously, haunting her with memories of Daniel. It was his theme, their theme, and now she could not remove its essence from her mind. She tried to close the box, yet the music played stronger and louder than before. She placed her hands over her ears in one last attempt to remove the pain from her soul. Yet all attempts were in vain. His very soul, which was now a large portion of her own, was in this piece of music, and in her mind they were inseparable. Her mind became flooded with thoughts of Daniel. Remembrance of times past, both happy and sorrowful, were being relived. Then suddenly, she heard his voice, "Josette, Josette, come to me". Again, the voice called out to her, this time louder than before, "Josette, Josette, come to me". She now knew what she must do.

*Chapter 9*

# A Man without Hope

Not unlike Josette, Daniel too greatly suffered with her departure. His mind knew that this was the way it must be, but his heart felt differently. Each forthcoming day brought an additional degree of emptiness, except for a flicker of hope that Josette might return. But with the passing of years even this flicker of hope was smothered by the cold wind of reality. He thought of leaving his wife and running to Josette's side, but he could not. It was not love that bound him to Priscilla, for the love between them had died many years ago. Now all his love was for Josette only. One would ask if not for love what other power on earth could bind two people together so tightly that neither one could break lose. The answer was simple, the conventions and expectations of society. Follow "till death do us part" and you shall be accepted without questions and be beyond reproach. Neglect this law and you shall live as a social outcast for the rest of the days of your life. Simple and straightforward, no more clearer a picture can be painted of what your life should be like. No personal liberties nor rights because you are society's child and bound by her standards and ideals. Such were the thoughts that haunted Daniel on many sleepless nights, yet both he and his wife believed and abided by these unwritten laws. They knew no other laws, no other lifestyle. They were taught well by their predecessors and they could not change now. They were husband and wife in name only, for appearances only. They had nothing in common and nothing to share. She deplored his music and never attempted to encourage the flourishment of his dream. He could not quite accept her lifestyle as it was during their marriage. Parties, dances, balls, the country club, social gatherings on every level, day in and day out. He found pleasure in the simple promises of life and nature, she did not.

He was too successful to alienate his supporters with an act of adultery and even divorce. They must appear to be happy so he can maintain his position at the Julliard School as "Dean of the Music Academy". The Board of Directors would not tolerate scandal. How would this aristocratic society, these families, the Board, react to an acting dean leaving his wife for a concert pianist who was a former student. Would they believe that he was not totally at fault and that sincere love was responsible for his actions? No, they would indeed call him an adulterer and forbid their children from attending his school. Accordingly, the attendance at his concerts would decline sharply. Both Daniel and Priscilla needed public opinion too much to dissolve their far less than perfect marriage, which had now become an agreement of convenience. She enjoyed his fame and the social life his fame constructed. She was so fitting for such a life of parties and would not give it up. He, on the other hand would not willingly abide by such a lifestyle. He did not quite like people of his own class and certainly did not wish to be around them all the time. He found these people to be superficial. What he loved about Josette was that she was real, not an image. Josette and Daniel shared one soul, one desire to live apart from the world they knew. No other woman he had met to date was so much like him. Josette could understand his feelings and desires. But now she is gone, and she has taken his soul, his heart with her. When Josette departed, she also took unintentionally his desire to live. For without her nearby, who would he confide in? Who would listen patiently and understand his sorrows? For a long time, he was an empty emotionless yet functioning being. Then Josette came and filled his heart with love which he believe he could never find again. Now that he has experienced the rapture of love, he no longer can live without it. His enthusiasm for life that Josette brought back to him was now gone. He hesitated to sleep at night for he could not bear the coming of the next morning. Prolonging the nights into days became his life now. Every day he would be more tired than the day before. He could not function any longer as a dean or a pianist. His dream of fame was his known reality and the only thing that could offer him the will to live. Yet that dream was no longer there to sustain him. In the years that Josette was gone he began to deteriorate as a man and as a public figure. His concerts became fewer with time. The great concert halls no longer wanted him inside their walls. He began to attend less and less the various academy social functions and those he did attend became a source of plenty of free alcohol. The more of an alcoholic he became the less socially acceptable he was. He lost many of his so-called friends. For if they were truly friends, they would have helped him in his hour of need. He even lost his dutiful wife and on socially acceptable grounds. "A divorce, of course, how would such a lady live in the same house with an alcoholic". Regardless of the fact that the house was so large (75 rooms in total) that she never had to see him at all. His den was in the left wing of the house and he would always be found there with either a glass in his hand or asleep in a drunken stupor. His leave of absence from the Academy secured him at least that position, assuming people would accept him back within their midst. For now, all knew of his drinking and he was a social outcast. It is curious how those who condemned his problem and openly stated that an alcoholic needs help, never attempted, nor for that matter, never even thought of helping Daniel. An alcoholic needs friends, understanding, compassionate people, now more than any other time in their life. To outcast him will not shame him into reforming but will reinforce his need to escape through alcohol. Shame, humiliation, and self-contempt drives an alcoholic deeper into this state until he reaches the point of no return. If someone had extended out their hand, one helping hand from even his dutiful wife was all he needed. But no one seemed to care. All scattered in countless directions, as far away as possible from him, leaving him alone to die surrounded by 75 empty rooms. The Charles M. Schwab House passed down to Daniel from his father was an extravagant, 75 room mansion located on Riverside Drive between West 73rd and West 74th Streets, on the Upper West Side in New York City. It was constructed for steel magnate Charles M. Schwab and was the grandest and most ambitious house ever built on the island of Manhattan. Daniel grew up in this house which his parents made into a home and it was now his refuge, but not for long. Priscilla was determined to ruin Daniel and indeed she did. Her divorce settlement forced him to sell his family home and give her half of the proceeds as well as most of his remaining assets. Daniel was in no condition to contest and as he sank deeper into his bottle of whiskey, he lost whatever assets were left and untouched by his loving wife. Daniel soon enough joined the countless number of souls living on the streets of New York City. Life on the streets of NYC was a challenge for Daniel at first. Soon he learned of the local shelters, sources of food and labor. Yet when he drank his ability to think clearly was highly impaired, he would not realize the cold and would have to depend on others to convince him to move indoors or to a shelter. Time on the streets had no delineation, no beginning, and no end. One day poured into the next creating one continuous existence. When Daniel was sober his priority was to find a safe place to sleep and sometimes that meant he needed to be creative. Some of them were typical, like parks, beaches, overpasses, or shelters, but others were less obvious. An airport such as JFK Airport which was his favorite, an abandoned car if the lot was not managed by security measures such as Doberman pinchers, an open train car in a trainyard or an open storage locker which gave the feeling of a bedroom without the furniture. As he was chased from one place, he would move to another with ease. The hardest issue Daniel faced as did all those living on the streets of NYC was getting injured. Accidents could happen but the homeless were often the bunt of anger and victims of violence. Abusing the homeless was not unusual because they were easy targets. Once injured it was hard to get any medical assistance. People would die from a lack of simple medical care that most of us take for granted. A cut, a broken bone, or an illness left untreated can become infected and deadly very quickly. Daniel quickly learned to protect himself he needed to band together with other homeless people. It was the code of survival on the street. Those on the streets would do their best to help each other out, share tips, and warn each other of potential danger. Nurses and doctors from local health facilities would often make the rounds to monitor the health of the occupants of the streets. Homeless people would create their own community. There were tent cities, homeless encampments, particularly in large cities such as New York. There is also a healthy barter system where you can trade for things you need without money. Life on the streets was life in a community with different boundaries. Daniel learned to keep a few necessary supplies, like his water and liquor bottles, some non-perishable foods, and a sleeping blanket, all of which he had to carry with him wherever he went. When he could, he would, sleep in a group or with another person for security. If he could not find someone he could trust, he would go to a shelter to see if they have any openings. To reduce the risk of danger, Daniel would sleep during the day at parks, open highly visible areas, with Central Park being his favorite. To get food and supplies, Daniel would ask churches and shelters for help. He would bathe himself on occasion when he would remember to do so in public restrooms and use spare change from begging to wash his clothes. Appearance mattered to Daniel when he was sober. When he was drinking, nothing mattered.

A pastor from a local church, St. Francis Xavier, Rev. Edward McCluskey, was familiar with the life on the streets. He too lived the life Daniel now lives. He was fortunate that a Bishop found him and brought him back into society and his calling. He received help for his drinking problem and has been sober for 10 years. Since then, he has helped many leave the streets and found work and shelter for them. His church is known as a refuge for the homeless, and Daniel would seek its assistance for food and shelter on cold nights. Father Edward, as Daniel would call him. recognized Daniel from his previous life and wished to help him back to sobriety. Every night Father Edward would roam the streets looking for those he could help. He would see to it that Daniel was in a safe space especially when he was very drunk and not responsible for his wellbeing. Father would take him into the church where he could give him a warm meal and a place to sleep in peace. He was Daniel's guardian angel and often Daniel had no idea the difference Father Edward made in preserving his life. Father Edward did not know the reason that Daniel drank so heavily but he did not care. He felt that if Daniel wished to share his past, he would. Father Edward only cared about giving Daniel a future. So, on this particular cold and snowy night, Father Edward brought Daniel once again into his warm and inviting church. The hot coffee and warm soup with bread was perfect for Daniel and he began to feel alive. Father Edward and Daniel talked for what seemed like hours and Daniel told Father about Josette and his past life. Father listened with much empathy and spoke of his own loss. He had been in love once many years ago. He loved his work as a pastor and had taken a vow of celibacy. A member of his parish was a young widow that needed his support. With time they became very close. If it were not for his vow of celibacy, he would have offered her marriage, but he could not. He was torn between his love for her and his vow. He found his solace, not unlike Daniel, in a bottle. Soon enough it became evident that he had become an alcoholic and lost everything of meaning, including the young widow. It took him a long time before he could return to his previous life. Daniel listened to Father Edward's story with caring and understanding. Both men were faced with moral decisions and they could not resolve them except through alcohol. Alcohol temporarily removed the need for a decision, at least so it appeared on the surface, but in many ways, it made the decision for them. As the temperature dropped outside and the men sat by the fireplace in the rectory for warmth, they realized they had much in common. Father Edward was determined to help Daniel more than ever and convinced Daniel to spend the night in one of the guest bedrooms in the rectory. The next morning Father Edward woke up early to make Daniel's favorite breakfast. He waited for Daniel to come downstairs into the dining area for several hours. Concerned he went up to the guest bedroom only to find the bed made and Daniel gone. An empty bottle was in the trash and a short note was on the desk. It was addressed to Father Edward and simply said "Father thank you for a warm meal and a bed to sleep in. Most of all thank you for your understanding, but you see Father I am a lost cause. I cannot be helped; I do not deserve to be helped. Father, I must return to the streets where I belong." It was signed, "with much gratitude, Daniel". Father Edward sat on the made bed and cried. The snow fell steadily that day and Daniel continued to walk through the empty white streets with little to protect him from the cold but his blanket. It was late that night when Daniel finally succumb to the cold and collapsed on the pavement. As he was going in and out of consciousness he cried out to Josette. "Josette, Josette, come to me", "Josette, Josette, come to me".

# Chapter 10

# The Path Home

The snow was coming down at a faster pace as the night progressed and the temperatures were dropping to well below freezing. Josette realized that the voice she heard was Daniel's voice and she knew what she must do, find him. Meanwhile, Father Edward was not willing to give up on Daniel. Three lines from a poem written by Dylan Thomas took over his thoughts almost as a mantra, not unlike a prayer, playing over and over again. It was as if he was trying to send to Daniel's mind and body the strength to fight the coming of death–

**"Do not go gentle into that good night,
Old age should burn and rave at close of day.
Rage, rage against the dying of the light."**

Both wandered the streets of the city looking desperately for one man under the fallen snow. Josette knew that Daniel was out there in the cold and it only served to increase her resolve. Father Edward knew Daniel's favorite places to sleep and began his search there. The winds were picking up and the snow fall was quickly becoming a blizzard. Josette could not let anything impede her search. Daniel's words resonated in her mind and she could hear them clearly spoken with desperation. Father quicken his footsteps for he felt Daniel's desperation to live. Josette saw in the distance a hand raised slightly above the snow on the pavement ahead. As she began to run to its position, she saw a man running towards the hand. They both arrived and realized that the hand belonged to Daniel. The hand was cold but not frost bitten. With strength and resolve both Josette and Father Edward dug through the snow to uncover a man unconscious and barely breathing. It was Daniel and his life was slipping away. Father Edward quickly picked him up and Josette covered him with the blankets she was carrying. Together they brought Daniel to the church. Josette held his cold hands and spoke to him while Father Edward called for assistance. The storm made it difficult for medical personnel, yet they appeared at the church eager to help. With the aid of all Daniel was transported to the local hospital. Josette and Father Edward stayed with Daniel during his transport. His hypothermia was serious, and frostbite did set into his extremities. As his body temperature was slowly increased the damage to his body was evident. Josette and Father Edward prayed together. Josette had not prayed for a very long time. She had memories of praying with her parents as a young child but barely remembered how. Father Edward held her hands in his, told her to close her eyes and tell God what was in her heart. Hours went by and there still was no word on Daniel. Josette began to cry feeling that she had lost the man she loved for so long. Father Edward, too, wanted this man to live. He pleaded with God to take his life in the place of this man's life. "Take me, Father", he said over and over again. It was the hours of early morning of the next day when the doctor came to see them. Daniel made it through the night, he was stable for now but still unconscious. The next 48 hours will determine if he will survive. Josette began to cry but unsure as to why. She was happy he was still with them but afraid as to what the next day would bring. Father Edward assured her that this was a good sign that he had made it through the night. He reassured her that he would be there with her over the many hours. She would not be alone. They exchanged a few words between them. He held her hand and that was all Josette needed. Both stayed with Daniel in his room. Josette held his hand and spoke gently to him. She spoke of the years they spent together, about those special moments. With every word she would look into his face for any reaction, any recognition of her voice, for any indication of life returning. His vitals were stable but his body, now warm, was still. She was determined to bring him back to her. He seemed determined to stay in his lonely existence. Father Edward also spoke with him hoping for some semblance of life. Yet no response. Forty-eight hours were gone, and Daniel did not emerge from his state of stillness. The doctor's prognosis went from positive to concerning. Yet Daniel's body was still and the hope that he would return was diminishing with every passing hour.

Father Edward had to return to his duties at his church but promised Daniel that he would return. It was the end of the third day and Josette began begging Daniel to awaken. She promised him a life together and at that moment she felt him squeeze her hand. At first, she thought she imagined it, that it was wishful thinking, but it happened again, this time with more strength than before. Her petite hand felt the pressure and she knew he was aware that she was beside him. Slowly his eyes opened, and he began to cry. She called for the nurse that came tunning in pleased at the scene. Father Edward had returned to the hospital and had been praying for Daniel in the hospital's Chapel. He suddenly felt a need to return to Daniel's room. Daniel looked at both Josette and Father Edward and a smile emerged. He was happy to see both and to know he was alive. It took a few more days before Daniel could speak and move his extremities the slightest but he was on the road to recovery and that is all that mattered.

Several weeks went by and with the help of trained medical personnel and the encouragement from Josette and Father Edward, Daniel began regaining the use of his arms and his legs.

Daniel was determined to improve his health and get through his alcohol dependency. He now had a reason to rebuild his life. It was an uphill and challenging battle but for the first time in a long time he knew what he must do and more so that he was not alone. Yet, alcohol dependency was very real for Daniel. He had physical and mental withdrawal symptoms after not drinking even for a short period. He found at first that the same amount of alcohol was needed to relieve his withdrawal symptoms. Initially he felt he had to drink to stop tremors or to cure a hangover. Alcohol dependency as experienced by Daniel was the need to drink alcohol often to function in one's daily life. Such was the case for Daniel each and every day. To survive each day, alcohol became his crutch, his lifeline. Alcohol dependency otherwise known as alcoholism consisted of four symptoms easily seen in Daniel. It expressed itself as a craving: a strong need, or compulsion, to drink or find a drink at all costs. Once drunk it was obvious that Daniel would lose control and have an inability to limit his drinking on any given occasion. Last and the most difficult to overcome was his physical dependency which was now emerging with withdrawal symptoms, such as nausea, sweating, shakiness and anxiety, the alcohol use was stopped after his many periods of heavy drinking. Rather than deal with the physical manifestations of withdrawal, Daniel chose to continue drinking. Daniel kept on drinking alcohol even when he knew it increased his risk for health problems. Health problems such as liver problems, stomach ulcers, high blood pressure, and stroke. After much time Daniel had developed a tolerance for alcohol. The amount of alcohol that Daniel did drink usually no longer caused the affects he desired. He needed to drink even more alcohol to get the same effect. He mentally craved alcohol. He began to have a desire to drink more often and to drink larger amounts of alcohol. He tried to quite on a few occasions but had problems managing his alcohol use. He was not able to control his drinking habits. He kept going back to drinking even after he quit. As he spend less time doing more important things, he lost total control of his life choices. He chose to spend much of his time drinking alcohol and associating with people who also drink. He began to have problems with social or daily activities at the academy and even his home life was affected. More and more he would choose events or activities that would include drinking. Daniel soon realized that he could not try to stop drinking on your own. Father Edward made arrangements for Daniel to be admitted to an inpatient facility for treatment of severe dependence to make sure he withdrew safely. He was given medicines to decrease his craving for alcohol and placed into a support group such as Alcoholics Anonymous. A psychiatrist was assigned for continuing therapy even after he left the hospital.

Daniel made a promise to himself, that if and when he had recovered, he would join Father Edward's effort to help those remaining on the streets. Everyone needs guidance to go beyond the dependency and rebuild their life. Having someone by your side not only to guide you but to encourage and believe in you is what makes it possible to break the vicious cycle of dependency. Daniel wished to be that person, the one that makes a difference. With time he planned to return to his music but for now this was to be his primary focus. Helping others suffering from alcohol dependency, not unlike himself, gave Daniel a greater purpose in life. Reaching out to those lost and leading them back was an honorable goal but it was important to Daniel that in doing so he preserved the individual's dignity. Helping for the sake of helping alone is simply not enough and often it is not warranted nor is it productive.

If a person chooses not to be helped then it would be best for the short term for all concerned to respect that wish. The hope is that one day this individual would reach out, and when they do and they are ready, you would be there for them. Father Edward as his mentor taught him well. An addicted individual must choose to get help. If help is imposed, it might drive the addicted individual into further severe addiction.

So Josette proposed to Daniel, but he turned her down. Daniel wished to propose marriage to Josette but not until he had succeeded in rebuilding his life. Then and only then could he have a life with her. Josette did not care as to Daniel's status, yet his pride did not let him proceed until his life returned to some sense of normalcy. She had put her musical career on hold to be there for him. He now was ready to take hold of the reins of his future journey and he wanted her to return to her international tour. Josette hesitated because in her heart she was afraid that Daniel would fail without her. She was being arrogant without realizing it but it was to be expected. She was not convinced at first although Daniel's insistence that he could control his dependency finally convinced her. Is it not an old adage that "once an addict, always an addict"? Indeed, true to some degree for Daniel would have to battle with his demons every day of his life. Maybe with time it would get easier, but the urges are strong and can easily reemerge. "Take one drink to get through the day" was always with him in his thoughts. The strength to get through the day could no longer come from a bottle but from within himself. Focusing his thoughts and energies not on getting through the day because that would indeed lead back to the bottle, but instead on living each day to the fullest for others. When you focus on others and their needs there is no time for self-pity and self-indulgences. A misstep backwards is not an indication that you have failed. It is your reaction and response to that backstep that determines your success in continuing to move forward. Daniel convinced Josette to return to the world's stage while he stayed in NYC. Father Edward was convinced that Daniel could help tremendously some of his most difficult cases. In particular he asked Daniel to work with David. David was a young man of 18 years that had been living on the streets since the age of 14 years. His both parents were opiate addicts and they forced him to leave his home although still a child. David learned to survive on the streets but had turned to alcohol for solace, to wipe out the pain of his current existence. Daniel knew in his heart and mind that he could help David. David led a risky life of selling his body for food and his soul to alcohol. This was his life on the streets. For the past four years of his young life, he knew no other. David never had a real childhood for he often took care of his parents. When they were sick, he cleaned up after them. He learned to cook to keep them fed. He would check on them often to make sure they did not overdose. He was the parent, the responsible one, and they were the children. Now living on the streets, he needed to take care of himself only which for David was an easier task. Addiction was the norm in his young life, he knew no other choice. He never attended school, played sports, nor had friends. If it was not for the kindness of a neighbor and his own natural curiosity, he would not have had any opportunities. Ms. Tuli Norman, a schoolteacher, taught David to read/write from a young age and become comfortable with math. He was an excellent student and loved to read anything Ms. Norman would give him. Being a young true educator, Ms. Norman made sure that David had his daily lessons and was properly fed. When David was kicked out Ms. Norman searched for him. She had hoped he would have turned to her for support, but he did not wish to impose, so he turned to the streets. She searched for him for over six months and soon enough determined that David did not wish to be found, which indeed was the case.

The saddest part of David's story was that his biological parents had no clue that they had thrown their son out of their lives, nor that they even had a son. With time their addictions led to their deaths for there no longer was someone who loved them to care for and worry about them. David never knew about their fate for they died in obscurity as John and Jane Doe on the streets of NYC. David continued his life in the same obscurity, no friends, no companions just clients, no one that cared. Daniel became his guide and with time his friend. David had no one that ever cared for him except for Ms. Norman. If it were not for her, he would have never learned to trusts adults and Daniel would not have been able to reach him. David did not wish to the live the life he saw his parents live, he wanted more. So, Daniel took on the responsibility of raising this young man, adopting him, and giving him a home. Eventually David was ready to obtain his GED. He applied to college and graduated Summa Cum Laude with a degree in medicine, his focus "addiction". Yet for every David in Daniel's life there was those that returned to the streets and he could not help, Daniel was determined to change their lives and did not give up on them, instead he watched over them and made the streets as safe as possible for them. Not unlike Father Edwards, Daniel became the "angel" of the streets and many trusted him in the hour of need to be there for them. Daniel was finally ready to return to the concert circuit and taught music to those on the streets of NYC at no cost from the basement of St. Francis Xavier.

Josette was finishing up her successful international tour and returned to NYC to be with Daniel. Both their lives were finally settled as Josette accepted a position to teach as part of the Academy of Music of the Julliard School.

This time when Josette proposed, Daniel accepted.